SUPER-CHARGED!

STUNT PLANES

BY

Rosemary Grimm

PUBLISHED BY

CRESTWOOD HOUSE

Mankato, MN, U.S.A.

CIP

LIBRARY OF CONGRESS CATALOGING IN PUBLICATION DATA

Grimm, Rosemary.
  Stunt planes.
  (Super-charged!)
  Includes index.
  SUMMARY: Describes the sport of stunt flying, including its history, the most popular
stunt planes, basic stunts, and stunt flying contests.
  1. Stunt flying—Juvenile literature.   [1. Stunt flying.]   I. Title.
TL711.S8G75   1988   797.5'4—dc19   87-29020
ISBN 0-89686-363-8

International Standard	**Library of Congress**
Book Number:	**Catalog Card Number:**
0-89686-363-8	87-29020

CREDITS

Cover: Frozen Images (Kurt Mitchell)
Department of the Navy: 36, 37, 39, 40-41
EAA: 16, 17, 30
Rosemary Grimm: 8, 20, 21, 31
The Bettmann Archives, Inc.: 24
Frozen Images: (Jim Braudenburg) 7: (Kurt Mitchell) 11, 15, 32
Third Coast Stock Source: (Alan Magayne-Roshak) 4, 9, 12-13; (Brent Nicastro) 22-23;
(Paul H. Henning) 43
FPG International: (D. C. Lowe) 26; (Dave Gleiter) 28-29
Globe Photos, Inc.: (Robert Rodvik) 18, 33, 34, 44

Produced by Carnival Enterprises.

CRESTWOOD HOUSE

Box 3427, Mankato, MN, U.S.A. 56002

TABLE OF CONTENTS

A pilot prepares for his first stunt.

INTRODUCTION

The stunt pilot, high in the air, glances down at the waving crowd. Even at a height of only a few thousand feet, he feels isolated from the earth.

A strong wind whips the pilot's hair as he double checks the gas gauge. The engine roars. The pilot releases the plane's smoke. He pulls back on the control stick and the plane flies upward. His first stunt, a huge loop in the sky, begins fast. The crowd vanishes and the pilot sees only blue sky.

As the plane curves upside down, the pilot feels a tug on his seat belt and harness. His body is lifted off his seat. He looks up and sees the audience upside down. He grins and waves.

The downward movement of the plane is strong as it completes its loop. The pilot puts his hand back on the control stick and pushes it forward. He is pressed hard against his seat. One more pull on the stick and the plane is level again. He flies low and hears the cheers of the crowd. The pilot has had a terrific ride, and the audience has seen a perfect loop!

THE BEGINNINGS OF STUNT FLYING

In 1917 the United States entered World War I, joining Great Britain and France, who had been fighting the war since 1914. Besides bringing fresh supplies and more soldiers, the U.S. also brought airplanes to replace the ones Great Britain and France had lost.

During the war, the pilots delivered supplies to soldiers and destroyed enemy buildings. As the pilots flew their planes through hostile territory, they discovered the best way to avoid attack. They could make their planes loop, twist, roll, and turn. These early stunts confused the enemy. Also, the pilots could escape bullets!

These stunts saved many pilots' lives. Fighter pilots began taking classes to learn more about stunt flying. Basic Battle Acrobacy was one course required for every fighter pilot.

BARNSTORMING

After the war, many fighter pilots were out of work, and many planes used in the war were for sale. Some of the pilots bought these planes and flew all over the country giving rides to people. Many people had never ridden in a plane before, so they paid the pilots to take them for a ride. The pilots who gave these rides were called barnstormers.

There were no airports and no mechanics for the barnstormers. They had to find their own landing spots and fix their own planes. The barnstormers had

Today's pilots enjoy the freedom of flying.

Modern-day wingwalkers prepare for the next show.

to keep their planes outside in all weather. The fabric on the wings easily rotted, and screws and joints were often rusted.

After a while, people wanted more than just an airplane ride. They wanted to see the planes perform in the air. They wanted to see the pilots do tricks. The barnstormers began performing their loops and twists in the air. They traveled from one state to another in the 1920's and performed at county fairs

Wingwalkers add excitement to any air show.

and city air shows. Two pilots would sometimes perform together in the air. The people loved this new way of flying!

To make their shows more exciting, the barnstormers asked some women to join their new act. Many of these women became wingwalkers. Wingwalkers walked on a plane's wings while the plane was flying. One of the early wingwalkers was Gladys Ingle. Gladys was not afraid to walk on a plane's wings as it flew. In one act she attached a target to the upper wing of her plane. As the plane flew, she shot arrows at the target as she stood on the upper wing!

But flying old airplanes in all kinds of weather — and walking on their wings — was dangerous. Many barnstormers crashed their planes as they tried to invent new stunts to attract audiences. The awful risks of barnstorming did not discourage new pilots, however. They still wanted to feel the thrill of flying!

THE FIRST STUNT PLANES

Gladys Ingle, and many of the barnstormers, flew the Curtiss JN-4D — nicknamed "The Jenny." The Jenny was built by Glen Curtiss in 1914. During and after World War I, 10,000 Jennies were built. When the war was over, these planes were sold to pilots at a very cheap price.

Because the Curtiss Jenny had two wings, it was called a biplane. One wing was above the pilot's cockpit, and the other wing was below. The pilot flew the Jenny from the back seat while his passenger sat in the front seat. The pilot always had the best view of the ground and sky.

But the Jenny had many problems. For one thing, it did not have any wheel brakes. The plane needed time to stop on its own. The pilot almost always had

This wingwalker is strapped securely to the top wing of a biplane.

to land in a huge field. Sometimes the planes hit
fences or ran into ditches when they landed. Then it
would take hours for the pilot to find a farmer with
a team of horses and haul his Jenny back onto the
field. Also, the Jenny could not fly very high. It flew
only 4,000 feet (1,219 meters) above the ground and
could not fly over high mountains.

Another popular stunt plane used during the
1920's was the J-1. The J-1 had been used to train
pilots during World War I. Over 1,600 J-1s were
built for the Army Air Service.

Like the Jenny, many of these planes were sold
after the war. The barnstormers used the J-1s in

many of their stunt flying acts. In the early 1920's, the J-1 was also used to teach students at flying schools.

WHAT MAKES A STUNT PLANE?

The structure of a stunt plane (the frame, the wings, and the tail) must be strong. A plane that can't withstand the pressures of a stunt might snap in half.

A stunt plane's controls must also be in perfect working order. A stunt plane has the same controls

To perform a perfect stunt, a plane's structure needs to be strong.

as a regular plane. The altimeter tells the pilot the plane's altitude (how high the plane is off the ground). The air speed indicator tells the pilot how fast the plane is moving. The tachometer tells the pilot how fast the engine is working. As the plane performs stunts, the engine must work harder. The tachometer alerts the pilot when there is too much strain on the engine. If there is too much strain, the engine could use up its gas supply too quickly.

The artificial horizon indicator is another important control in the cockpit. On the face of this control is a horizon line. When the pilot flies the

plane level with the ground, the control's indicator stays level on the artificial horizon. When the pilot dips one wing to the left, the indicator also dips to the left. The stunt pilot relies on this control when he is performing any type of stunt. He checks the artificial horizon to make sure he is flying straight after each stunt.

Before each flight, the pilot needs to inspect his plane to be sure it is in safe condition. This inspection is very important. The pilot tightens all screws on the plane. He checks the gasoline and oil levels and all his controls. Everything must be in perfect condition. Finally, the pilot checks for any loose equipment. If something is not packed right, it could drop out of the plane during a loop or spin!

REQUIRED EQUIPMENT

The Federal Aviation Board passes laws that all pilots must obey. One part of the law states that stunt pilots must use certain equipment. One of the most important pieces of equipment is the parachute. Because the cockpit, or pilot's seat, is very small, special parachutes are used that can be folded into a tiny bundle. The pilot straps on the parachute and sits on it. The parachute will not get in his way while he is flying—but it is ready if he should need it!

The shoulder harness is a must for any stunt plane.

A good stunt pilot can fly his plane in any direction.

The harness has five straps. Two straps are seat belts. One strap is brought up between the pilot's legs and secured at his waist. The last two straps are brought over the pilot's shoulders.

A harness is most important when the plane is flying upside down. It keeps the pilot from falling out of his seat! It also keeps him from being pushed forward into the controls during a stunt.

Other equipment includes a helmet, goggles, and gloves. The helmet protects the pilot's head in case of an accident. The goggles are important in an open

The Pitts Special was designed for stunt flying.

cockpit. They allow the pilot to see clearly even when the wind is blowing in his face. The gloves give the pilot a firmer grip on the controls.

THE PITTS SPECIAL

Not all planes are stunt planes. And not all stunt planes can perform all stunts. There are certain planes that are very good at performing stunts. These

The Special is a short, lightweight stunt plane.

planes are used for training pilots, for air shows, and for everyday stunt flying.

The Pitts Special is known throughout the world as a popular stunt plane. It was designed by Curtis Pitts in 1942. The Pitts Special is solidly built and performs most stunts very well.

The Special is a small biplane with an open cockpit. A standard Pitts Special is only about 15 feet

These pilots make stunt flying look easy.

or 4.5 meters long (about the length of a large pickup truck). Its wing span is only about 17 feet (5 meters) long. The airplane weighs between 700 and 1,150 pounds (315 to 520 kilograms), depending upon the type of equipment it has (an average lightweight plane weighs about 3,000 pounds or 1,360 kilograms).

In 1949, a well-known stunt pilot named Betty Skelton began to fly a Pitts Special called the "Li'l

Stinker." She flew the "Li'l Stinker" in a contest in London, England.

"The reaction to 'Li'l Stinker' was astounding," Betty said after her flight. "I think it was about the smallest airplane flying at the time...they just fell in love with it."

In the 1950's and 1960's, Pitts improved the engine and cockpit of the Pitts Special. He studied British and Russian planes. He made the cockpit bigger and the engine more powerful. Then in 1972, the U.S. Aerobatic Team won the World Aerobatic Championship using Pitts Specials. That was the best year for Curtis Pitts and his airplane!

The Pitts Special can be bought either fully assembled or in a kit form. Pilots must have their kit planes tested for strength before they can be flown.

A stunt pilot can perform stunts easily in a Pitts Special. It flies as well upside down as it does right side up. The Pitts Special is tough and won't break apart when flying difficult stunts.

OTHER POPULAR STUNT PLANES

The Christen Eagle, like the Pitts Special, was specifically designed for stunt flying. It is strong and reliable. According to one pilot, the Christen Eagle

The Cessna is a stunt plane that is easy to fly.

has "excellent manners on the ground and in the air."

The Eagle is a biplane that is usually painted white with bright blue, red, and gold eagle feathers. It was designed by Frank Christensen in the early 1970's. He studied the best parts of the Pitts Special and tried to make his plane better. The Eagle ended up being bigger, faster, and more powerful than the Pitts Special. The Eagle has a top speed of 184 miles per hour (mph) or 290 kilometers per hour (km/h) and can climb 2,100 feet (640 meters) in one minute.

The Christen Eagle is a brightly-painted plane.

The Cessna 172 Skyhawk is another popular stunt plane. It first flew in 1955. Since then, more pilots have bought it than any other light airplane. One pilot described the Skyhawk as "a willing workhorse that's as comfortable as an old shoe."

The Skyhawk is a monoplane, meaning it has only one wing located over the cockpit. The Cessna Company built the Skyhawk for inexperienced pilots. Many new pilots say that the Skyhawk is "as easy to handle on the ground as a car."

The Eagles Aerobatic Team pilots fly their Christen Eagles with amazing skill.

The Skyhawk is often used to train stunt pilots. More powerful planes, however, are needed for advanced stunt flying.

The Stearman Model 75 has been around a long time, and it's still a popular biplane. During World War II the Model 75 was used to train new pilots. It

Pilots have flown the dependable Stearman since World War II.

was very strong, easy to fly, and very stable. New pilots quickly learned the instruments of the Stearman. After the war thousands of Model 75s were converted to crop dusting planes, and with every passing year they become more valuable to collectors.

The North American AT-6 is an Air Force plane that can be used for stunt flying — although that was not why it was designed. The first AT-6 was built in 1935. During World War II, the plane was used to train advanced pilots ("AT" means Advanced Trainer). Advanced pilots already knew how to fly smaller aircraft. They were ready to fly a plane with more instruments — and more power!

This powerful aircraft has many nicknames. Navy pilots called it the SNJ. The pilots in Canada called it the Harvard. Other people called it the Texan.

The AT-6 is a two-seater monoplane. Covering the cockpit is a huge plastic bubble supported by metal frames. The pilot sits in the front seat of the cockpit, which in this plane has the best view of the sky and ground. The passenger sits in back.

During training, the passenger was often the fighter pilot's teacher. One part of a pilot's training was learning how to fly using only instruments. The student sat in the back seat of the cockpit and the teacher sat in the front seat. The back seat was covered with canvas so the student could not see outside; he had to rely only on his instruments to fly. His teacher sat with a good view, ready to take over the controls in case his student ran into any trouble!

A formation of antique SNJs.

After the war many AT-6s were sold to pilots for the low price of $1,000 and used for stunt flying.

A HUGE CIRCLE IN THE SKY

A stunt is a change in the airplane's position; it does not happen by accident. In any stunt the pilot is always in control.

Most stunts are performed very high in the sky because the stunt pilot needs a lot of room. Only well-trained pilots fly at low altitudes.

The straight line, which is a part of every stunt, must be perfected before any other stunt is learned. In contests, the stunt pilot must begin and end his stunt by flying his plane in a straight line. Once he can fly perfectly straight, he is ready to learn other stunts.

The Loop, which is a huge circle in the sky, is another basic stunt. The pilot starts his Loop by pulling back on the control stick. The nose of the plane flies upward and the pilot is pushed into his seat. As the pilot flies upward, all he sees are clouds.

In a Loop, "the ground quickly disappears beneath the rising nose," says one stunt pilot, "and you must now keep your eye on the wings." As long as the wings are even, the plane is flying straight up.

This Stearman biplane is ready for another show.

28

Before he learns any stunt, a pilot must be able to fly perfectly straight.

At the top of the Loop, the plane is upside down and the pilot can again see the ground. He's halfway through his Loop!

The plane flew straight up the Loop, and it now must fly straight down — until it reaches the altitude where the Loop began. The Loop is finished!

The Loop, says one pilot, "makes you feel absolutely alone and free as you are carried higher

A stunt pilot uses smoke to trace his Loop.

and higher. You approach the feeling known only by those few who have actually left the earth."

A perfect Loop in the sky is not always easy to make. Sometimes the pilot makes an egg-shaped Loop or he loses his place and doesn't finish his circle.

The Loop teaches the stunt pilot to watch his speed and to always know his position in the sky.

OTHER BASIC STUNTS

Another stunt is Inverted Flight, which simply means flying the plane upside down! The pilot turns the plane until it is upside down and its wings are level with the ground.

The pilot cannot fly inverted for a long time. When the pilot flies upside down, all his blood rushes to his head. If he stays like this for too long, he will black out and lose control of his plane.

It's always exciting to see a stunt plane fly upside down!

A formation of stunt planes perfoms the Slow Roll.

The Slow Roll may look easy to do from the ground, but there are many things that a pilot must keep in mind. Performing the Slow Roll means flipping the plane around and around while flying in a straight line. The pilot must keep the plane level, keep it flying straight, and roll it continuously, all at the same time. That's not easy!

This stunt is difficult also because the pilot is not firmly in his seat all the time. At one point in the

From the ground, the Wingover looks like a huge upside-down "U".

Slow Roll, the plane is flying inverted. This pushes the pilot away from his seat. The pilot has his harness on, but he also gets pushed away from his controls. He must hold on tight to his control stick at all times.

The Slow Roll teaches the stunt pilot how to think ahead, how to use the controls, and how to coordinate a stunt. It is meant to be flown smoothly, with no jerky movements — and that takes much practice. But the whole stunt is completed in less than 15 seconds!

The Wingover is a more advanced stunt. It is a large, upside-down "U" in the sky. The stunt plane flies straight upward. At the "U's" highest point, the pilot turns the plane sharply. The plane then flies straight downward. The stunt ends when the plane is at the same altitude where it began. A student can't learn this stunt until he can do the other basic stunts.

THE BLUE ANGELS: NAVY FLIGHT TEAM

In the early days of stunt flying, military planes were used. These planes were well built. They were always available. In the 1930's and '40's, the air services of several nations organized stunt teams with their planes. They wanted a team of pilots who could fly stunts with the military planes. The U.S. Navy Flight Demonstration Squadron, known as the Blue Angels, is one of these teams.

The Blue Angels began in 1946. Their blue and yellow jet aircrafts have been seen by 168 million people! The team flies in 80 shows every year, from March to November. The Blue Angels, like many flight teams, are known for their skill and their many breathtaking flights. The Blue Angels perform their air show stunts at very high speeds.

The squad of seven pilots are selected from Navy

Two F-18 Hornets perform the Blue Angels' Fortus Maneuver.

or Marine Corps pilots. The chosen pilots fly with the Blue Angels for two years. The rookie pilots learn much from the veteran pilots who have been on the team longer.

The Blue Angels squad leader flies the number one position. During air shows, the seventh pilot stays on the ground and describes the stunts to the crowd. The team performs loops, rolls, and tight formations (a formation is several planes flying very close together).

F-18 Hornets fly in the Diamond Formation.

The Diamond is the Blue Angels' most well-known formation. They need four planes to make the Diamond. The lead plane flies first. Close behind it are two planes flying side by side. The two planes are centered behind the leader. The last plane is behind them. He centers his plane between the two planes in the middle.

The pilots must always keep their eyes on the other team planes. In all formations, the planes fly very close to each other. In the Diamond formation, the planes fly only 36 inches apart! The pilots must keep a firm hand on the controls. They must all fly at the same speed.

Only two planes are needed to perform a popular Blue Angels' air show stunt — The Fortus Maneuver. In this stunt, one plane flies above the other. Suddenly, the top plane flips and flies upside down. The top plane inches forward until it is directly above the bottom plane. The bottom pilot can look up and see the cockpit of the other plane. The spellbound crowd cheers!

From 1974 to 1986 the Blue Angels flew the A-4 Skyhawk. It was a small but powerful aircraft that was first flown in 1955. The A-4 sat only one person, but weighed 11,000 pounds (4,990 kilograms)! The Skyhawk was reliable and the pilots didn't need to worry about the engines failing. The Skyhawk was a strong jet, so it could perform many different stunts.

In 1987 the Blue Angels replaced the A-4 with the F-18 Hornet. The naval officers thought that the A-4 was getting too old. They wanted the Blue Angels to fly a modern aircraft.

The F-18, which first flew in 1979, can fly up to 600 mph (960 km/h). It can fly at higher altitudes than the A-4. It can also turn around more quickly.

On a clear day the F-18 can fly as high as 7,000 feet (2,133 meters). From this height the planes can do dazzling stunts and formations, and still be seen by the audience on the ground. If the weather is

Two Blue Angels' aircraft fly within inches of each other.

cloudy, this jet can fly as low as 400 feet (121 meters).

The Blue Angels practice from January to March at the Naval Air Facility in El Centro, California. This area of California is known for its dry conditions. The Blue Angels can practice many weeks without having to stop because of rain.

Each morning the pilots talk about the stunts and formations they will practice. The rest of the day is spent flying. At the end of the day, they talk about how they can improve their performance. The pilots want their stunts and formations to be perfect for every air show.

An air-to-air view of the powerful A-4 Skyhawks.

STUNT FLYING CONTESTS

Stunt flying was growing so popular that in 1970 a new organization, the International Aerobatic Club (IAC), was started. The IAC knew that stunt pilots wanted to compete against each other, so they set up the International Aerobatic Championships. The contest is held each year in Fond du Lac, Wisconsin.

To enter the contest, a pilot must have an airplane that can perform many types of stunts. The most popular plane used is a Pitts Special. The pilots must show the judges their pilot certificates. Then all the planes are inspected.

There are five judges who watch the stunt pilots from the ground. The pilots must fly within The Box, which is an imaginary cube in the air, like the strike zone in baseball. The Box is 3,300 feet (1,005 meters) long and 3,300 feet wide. At the top, The Box is 3,500 feet (1,066 meters) off of the ground. Markers on the ground tell the pilots where The Box is located. The pilots get points for each stunt and for staying within The Box. The pilot with the most points at the end of the day wins the trophy.

In an aerobatic contest, pilots enter one of four categories depending on their skill. An inexperienced pilot would enter the contest in a lower category. An experienced pilot would enter in

A stunt pilot needs all his skill to win a stunt flying contest.

Stunt planes can do just about anything!

an upper one. But no matter what category the pilot enters, he must perform certain stunts and tests of his skill.

Each pilot performs a free program, which is a set of stunts that he makes up. He tries to impress the judges with loops and rolls. There is also an Unknown Program to be tackled. The Unknown Program is a set of stunts given to each pilot 30 minutes before his flight. The pilot has no time to practice; he must practice "flying" the stunts in his head. His first try at this set of stunts is for the judges. To do an Unknown Program, a pilot must know many types of stunts. In the hardest class, the

Unknown Program is full of twists, double rolls, and many loops.

The more experienced pilot often flies as low as 300 feet (91 meters) off the ground!

THE FUTURE OF STUNT FLYING

Companies that build small biplanes and monoplanes have learned much from stunt planes. As stunt flying became more popular, pilots needed better controls for doing larger loops and smoother rolls. The companies improved the controls. The pilots needed stronger plane structures. The designers worked to improve the overall strength of these planes.

Pilots have also learned much from flying their stunt planes. The pilot knows about every part of his plane. He knows what can go wrong, and he learns how to avoid problems. He has learned to handle his plane in all situations.

The next time a stunt plane shoots by in the sky, look up at the pilot and you'll see a person who has challenged himself. He or she has learned to fly in a way that most people only dream about. Stunt pilots can do amazing things with their planes — and they'll continue to dream up harder stunts to dazzle wide-eyed audiences.

FOR MORE INFORMATION

For more information on stunt planes, stunt flying contests, or any other type of plane write to:
The Experimental Aircraft Association (EAA)
Wittman Field
Oshkosh, WI 54903

GLOSSARY/INDEX

AEROBATICS 19, 42 — *Performing stunts in the air with an airplane; another term for "stunt flying."*

AIR SPEED INDICATOR 13 — *The instrument that tells the pilot how fast the plane is flying.*

ALTIMETER 13 — *The instrument that tells the pilot the plane's altitude.*

ALTITUDE 13, 27, 30, 35, 38 — *How high the plane is off the ground.*

ARTIFICIAL HORIZON 13, 14 — *The instrument that tells the pilot if the plane is level to the ground.*

BARNSTORMERS 6, 8, 9, 10, 11 — *Pilots who gave rides and performed stunts for people all over the country during the 1920's.*

BIPLANE 10, 17, 20, 24, 45 — *An airplane with two wings. One wing is located over the cockpit, and the other is located under it.*

BOX 42 — *In an aerobatic contest, The Box is an invisible cube in the air where the pilot must perform his stunts.*

COCKPIT 10, 13, 14, 16, 17, 19, 21, 25, 38 — *The seat in an airplane where the pilot sits.*

CONTROL STICK 5, 27, 34 — *The instrument used by the pilot to move the plane up, down, left, and right.*

CROP DUSTING 25 — *Using an airplane to spray chemicals onto crops to kill bugs and weeds.*

GLOSSARY/INDEX

FORMATION 36, 37, 38, 39 — *Two or more planes flying close together as they perform stunts.*

HARNESS 5, 14, 15, 34 — *A series of belts that strap the pilot and passengers into their seats.*

INVERTED FLIGHT 32, 34 — *To fly upside down.*

LOOP 5, 6, 8, 27, 30, 31, 36, 45 — *An aerobatic stunt performed by making a huge circle in the sky.*

MONOPLANE 21, 25, 44, 45 — *An airplane with one wing that is located either above the cockpit or below it.*

SLOW ROLL 6, 33, 34, 36, 44, 45 — *An aerobatic stunt performed by rolling the plane around and around while it is flying in a straight line.*

TACHOMETER 13 — *The instrument that tells the pilot how fast the airplane engine is turning over.*

UNKNOWN PROGRAM 44, 45 — *In an aerobatic contest, the Unknown Program is a set of stunts given to a pilot before he flies. The pilot has no time to practice the set.*

WINGOVER 35 — *An aerobatic stunt performed by flying the plane straight up, making a sharp turn, then flying straight down.*

WINGWALKER 9, — *A person who performs on an airplane's wing or body as the plane is flying.*